REBEKAH BALLAGH

This is Flo.

Can you give her a

BIG

wave hello?

Flo is going to school today – but she needs your help!

Flo is getting ready.
Let's help her pack her schoolbag.

Here's the list of things
Flo needs to take.

Flo gets to school and ... uh oh ... her best friend isn't here today! She looks so DISAPPOINTED.

Can you help Flo relax and settle in with some 5-finger breathing?

Trace your finger along the dotted lines of Flo's hand. Breathe in as you trace up her finger and breathe out as you trace down.

And look, Flo has found some
new friends to play with.

In the classroom it's time for writing. But, oh dear, Flo can't find her pencil.

She looks a little stressed.

It helps Flo concentrate when she stops to clear her mind.

Can you help Flo focus by looking around the classroom and finding 5 things that are green?

Good spotting!

Sometimes you just need to take a moment to find your

CALM...

Now Flo has remembered where she put her pencil!

Can you spot it?

Time for lunch, but, oh no . . . out in the playground a kid is annoying Flo.

She holds up her hand.

"Stop it, I don't like it!"

Flo feels **ANGRY**. Can you turn the page to teach Flo a handy tool to find her calm?

Let's teach Flo how to let out her anger safely.
Can you take a deep breath in,

SQUEEZE

your hands into fists, nice
and tight . . . and hold for

5 — 4
3 2
1

After lunch it's time for art.

Flo is trying to paint a tree but there's no green!

Can you help Flo by mixing together the two colours that make green with your finger?

It's time to go home. Flo's mum is waiting to walk with her, but poor Flo can't tie her shoelaces.

Mum spies 3 cats.
Can you spot them too?

Back at home, Flo helps to make dinner. Dad reads the recipe and asks Flo to fetch carrots, tomatoes and cheese.

Look inside the fridge. Can you remember what Flo's dad asked for? Point to the ingredients they need.

Nice job! Dinner's done and it looks delicious.

Can you  on Flo's dinner to help cool it down?

Can you scrub Flo's toothbrush back and forth and up and down to give her teeth a good clean?

Yay, you found Ted!

Flo looks snug as a bug
and ready for sleep.

Thank you for helping Flo today.

Let's wish Flo a peaceful sleep.
Can you blow her a kiss goodnight?

Sweet dreams and sleep tight.

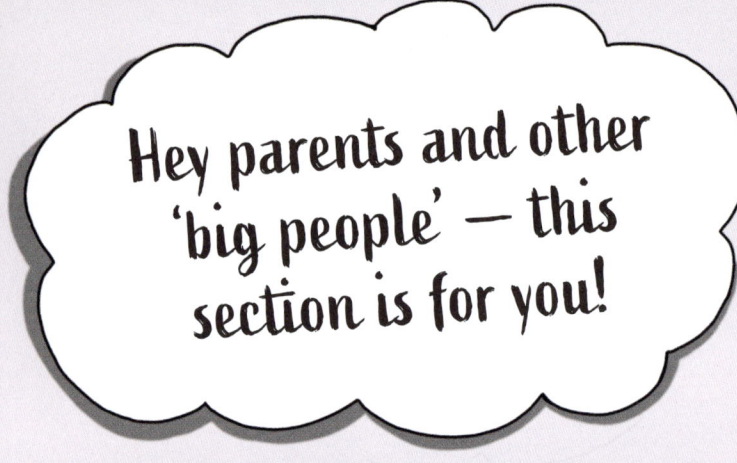

Executive function

Throughout *Let's Go, Flo!*, we looked at many different executive function skills. In this section we'll dive in to learn more about what this means and how you can support your little ones to develop these skills.

Executive function is like a manager inside our brains. The skills and processes involved allow us to set goals, plan, adapt, get things done and manage our emotions and impulses. When we struggle with executive function it impacts all areas of our lives, from school to home. Executive function skills help our brain to get going on a task, filter out distractions, and control emotions and impulses.

Executive function covers a range of different skills and processes. See the table below.

How can adults support kids to develop their executive function skills?

Executive function begins to develop early in life, aided by the warm and safe relationships kids experience with important adults around them — like you! Secure relationships and attachments lead to strong social-emotional development and executive function skills.

These skills can be developed and supported at any age, and especially when children are young. As adults, we can teach these skills through our relationships with them; by modelling what these skills look like (as we so often instinctually do when we narrate our actions during a task and what we need to do to get it done), through play and through teaching tools and games, by establishing routines, by breaking down big tasks into small chunks and by encouraging imagination and flexible thinking.

Executive function skills develop rapidly between 3–5 years of age but they take lots of time, practice and patience to develop. All kids are different and develop at different paces.

Some kids struggle with executive function skills. This does not make them a bad kid (there are no bad kids!) although their behaviours may be challenging. Helping kids to develop their executive function skills happens in a safe supportive relationship and environment, through modelling, teaching and nurturing (rather than punishing the tricky behaviours).

Executive Function:	What it means:	Examples from Flo:
Working memory	The ability to hold information in your mind to complete a task	Flo forgot where she had put her pencil in her writing lesson. She had to remember the recipe ingredients while cooking with Dad. She had forgotten where she put her bear at bedtime.
Attention and focus	The ability to stay present and on task	Flo lost her focus at the start of the writing lesson in class. She had to pay attention and focus to play 'I spy' with her mum on the walk home. She had to pay attention to her dad as they cooked dinner.

Inhibition and emotional regulation/control	The ability to stop a behaviour at the appropriate time and the ability to modulate emotional responses	Flo had to manage her disappointment at her friend being away from school. She had to manage her anger when she was being annoyed on the playground. She had to manage fear when she went to bed at night.
Organisation and planning	The ability to keep things in order and to manage a future-oriented task	Flo had a visual list of things she needed to pack in her schoolbag. Flo had lost her pencil for her writing lesson. Flo and her dad had to be organised to make dinner. Flo used a visual timer to help with brushing her teeth.
Task initiation and completion	The ability to begin a task and to stick to the task, problem-solving or generating ideas along the way	Flo had to use this skill when starting her writing lesson, during art class and to cook dinner with her dad.
Mental flexibility	The ability to move from one task to another and adapt to change	Flo had to adapt when she realised her friend wasn't at school and she had to get creative when there was no green paint.
Self-monitoring	Keeping track of what you are doing/monitoring your own performance and how you are feeling	Flo demonstrated this when she realised she couldn't tie her shoelaces and needed help. She demonstrated this every time she checked in with herself to identify how she was feeling (for example her fear let her know she needed her night light, her anger let her know she needed to use calm-down tools). She used a timer to monitor her teeth brushing at night.

Let's explore some ideas and fun ways to support the development of executive function in kids

Developing working memory

- make lists (like Flo's school list)
- play memory games like pairs, or set up a tray with a few different objects then have the child close their eyes. Remove one object from the tray, then the child opens their eyes and tries to remember which object is missing.
- the holiday packing game — one person starts 'When I go on holiday I take my swimsuit.' The next says, 'When I go on holiday I take my swimsuit and my toothpaste' — continue around the circle, each person adding an item to the list until someone can no longer remember the list.

Developing attention and focus

- play games like 'Simon says'
- play copy games — copy the action(s) of a partner or try mirror games (one person leads actions and the other tries to mirror/copy them at the same time)
- make up a dance routine to a favourite song
- play 'I spy'
- play 'what changed here' — one child stands in front of a group of others, then all kids close their eyes, an adult changes something about the child (i.e. undo a shoelace, put the hat back to front etc), then see if the kids can pick the difference
- play memory games (like pairs or the memory tray game)
- play 'make my shape' — get 4 different coloured Lego blocks and put a screen between you and the child (or between two children). One person makes a colour pattern with the Lego (i.e. yellow, red, blue, green) and instructs their partner step by step on which positions the blocks go in (i.e. 'put the red on top of the yellow'). Without being able to see, following instruction only, the partner tries to create the pattern.

Developing inhibition and emotional regulation/control

- exercise and movement — try walking to and from school like Flo and her mum, or play a game together
- teach emotional regulation skills (like the squeeze and shake or 5-finger breathing)
- teach kids how to name their feelings — my book *Big Feelings* is a good resource to explore this further
- practise calming and grounding strategies (like Flo did when she looked for 5 green things)
- play games where you have to freeze when the music stops

Developing organisation and planning

- create a visual timetable of the activities for the day
- plan and prepare a meal like Flo and her dad did
- have visual timetables of the bed or pre-school routine
- have a list of things to pack in their bag
- play 'beat the timer' — start a timer or a song and have kids complete a task by the time it finishes (i.e. packing up their toys, unpacking their school bag)
- use timers for activities that need to be time-limited like computer/TV time
- try '1 out, 1 in' with toys — kids need to put away toys that are out before taking out another one
- break tasks down into small chunks — give 1 or 2 instructions at a time
- encourage kids to put things back in the same place after they use them

Developing task initiation and completion

- use visual plans/timetables
- create a schedule or list of chores (age dependent)
- exercise or play a game to get energy out before starting a task
- use countdown timers to show when a task begins
- brainstorm the task together
- model and cue children with verbal reminders and demonstration of a task

Developing mental flexibility

- play 'fortunately, unfortunately' — the adult starts with a random scenario like 'I was getting ready to go to the beach' and then says, 'Unfortunately . . .' and adds something that might go wrong (e.g. 'we couldn't find our swimsuits' or 'there was an elephant in the driveway blocking the garage!') Then the child has a turn and thinks of something that could work instead, starting with 'Fortunately . . .' (i.e. 'fortunately, we decided we could swim in old clothes' or 'fortunately, we had some peanuts to lure the elephant out of the way'). The adult or the next kid continues with 'Unfortunately . . .'
- model going with the flow and changing plans suddenly
- try new things often and model getting out of your comfort zone (i.e. try new food, walk a new route home from school together, play a new sport, listen to new kinds of music etc)
- improvisation prop game — get a random object from your house and have fun creating all kinds of different uses for it (i.e. a bowl becomes a hat, a mushroom in the garden, a steering wheel for a car etc)
- play 'what am I' guessing games — e.g. give 3 clues to describe an animal and see if kids can guess what it is
- play puzzles, mazes etc

Developing self-monitoring

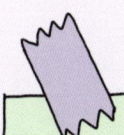

- model asking questions and asking for help, and explain why we are doing things
- check-ins — ask kids how they are doing as they are working on a task
- play games like Jenga
- play freeze dance — music stops and kids freeze
- talk about ways we can manage big feelings

More ways to have fun with this book — for kids!

- go back to page 10/11 — take a look around. Name 5 things you can see, 4 things you think Flo could touch that might feel interesting, 3 things you think Flo might be able to hear, 2 things you think Flo might smell and then 1 thing Flo might be able to taste (you can play this again on page 22/23)
- go back to page 22/23 — how many things can you spot on this page that start with the letter C? Can you spot something that doesn't belong in this picture? Can you spot the hidden bumble bee?

Some questions to ask kids for further exploration

Page 4/5 — What else do you think Flo should take to school? What about if it was raining? What would she need if she was going swimming?

Page 6/7 — What would you do if you got to school and your friend was away? What could you do if you saw another kid at school who looked lonely or sad?

Page 10/11 — What could Flo do to make it easier to find her pencil next time? What do you do to remember where your things are?

Page 14/15 — What could you do if someone was annoying you on the playground? What could you do if you saw someone at school who was being bullied?

Page 16/17 — How did you feel after doing the squeeze/shake? When could you use it?

Page 18/19 — What other colours can you mix together to make a new colour? What would happen if you mixed blue and red?

Page 22/23 — How many people can you count in this picture? What season do you think it might be and why? Do you think the boy on the bike is being safe and why or why not?

Page 26/27 — What fruit can you see? What veggies can you spot?

Page 28/29 — What's your night time routine?

Page 30/31 — What could Flo do to make it easier to find her teddy next time? Do you have a special toy you like to take to bed?

Page 32/33 — What helps you feel better if you feel scared?

Page 34/35 — What was your favourite part of your day today?

First published in 2023

Text and images © Rebekah Ballagh, 2023

All rights reserved. No part of this book may be reproduced or transmitted in any form or by any means, electronic or mechanical, including photocopying, recording or by any information storage and retrieval system, without prior permission in writing from the publisher.

Allen & Unwin
Level 2, 10 College Hill, Freemans Bay
Auckland 1011, New Zealand
Phone: (64 9) 377 3800
Email: auckland@allenandunwin.com
Web: www.allenandunwin.co.nz

83 Alexander Street
Crows Nest NSW 2065, Australia
Phone: (61 2) 8425 0100

A catalogue record for this book is available from the National Library of New Zealand.

ISBN 978 1 99100 602 8

Text design by Kate Barraclough
Set in Lunchbox Slab, Brandon Text, Active and Blaue Brush
Printed and bound in China by 1010 Printing Limited

10 9 8 7 6 5 4 3 2 1